DR. SEUSS

IMAGINATIVE CHILDREN'S BOOK WRITER AND ILLUSTRATOR

JENNIFER LANDAU

Britannica
Educational Publishing

IN ASSOCIATION WITH

ROSEN
EDUCATIONAL SERVICES

Published in 2016 by Britannica Educational Publishing (a trademark of Encyclopædia Britannica, Inc.) in association with The Rosen Publishing Group, Inc.
29 East 21st Street, New York, NY 10010

Distributed exclusively by Rosen Publishing.
To see additional Britannica Educational Publishing titles, go to rosenpublishing.com.

First Edition

Britannica Educational Publishing
J. E. Luebering: Director, Core Reference Group
Mary Rose McCudden: Editor, Britannica Student Encyclopedia

Rosen Publishing
Kathy Kuhtz Campbell: Senior Editor
Nelson Sá: Art Director
Nicole Russo: Designer
Cindy Reiman: Photography Manager
Bruce Donnola: Photo Researcher

Library of Congress Cataloging-in-Publication Data

Landau, Jennifer, 1961-
Dr. Seuss : imaginative children's book writer and illustrator / Jennifer Landau. -- First edition.
    pages cm. — (Britannica Beginner Bios)
 Includes bibliographical references and index.
 ISBN 978-1-68048-258-4 (library bound) — ISBN 978-1-5081-0063-8 (pbk.) — ISBN 978-1-68048-316-1 (6-pack)
 1. Seuss, Dr.—Juvenile literature. 2. Authors, American—20th century--Biography—Juvenile literature. 3. Illustrators—United States—Biography—Juvenile literature. 4. Children's stories—Authorship—Juvenile literature. I. Title.
 PS3513.E2Z726 2016
 813'.52—dc23
 [B]

2015014475

Manufactured in the United States of America

Photo credits: Cover, pp. 1, 8, 22 Universal History Archive/UIG/Getty Images; pp. 4, 5, 14, 21 Gene Lester/Archive Photos/Getty Images; p. 6 Cyrus McCrimmon/The Denver Post/Getty Images; pp. 10, 16, 18 John Bryson/The LIFE Images Collection/Getty Images; p. 11 © AP Images; p. 13 Courtesy of Dartmouth College Library; p. 20 © AF archive/Alamy; p. 23 Leonard McCombe/The LIFE Picture Collection/Getty Images; p. 24 William Foley/The LIFE Images Collection/Getty Images; p. 25 Betty Galella/Ron Galella Collection/Getty Images; p. 26 Tim Sloan/AFP/Getty Images; p. 27 William B. Plowman/Getty Images; p. 28 Joe Raedle/Getty Images; interior pages background graphic davorana/Shutterstock.com.

CONTENTS

CHAPTER ONE

WHO WAS DR. SEUSS?

Theodor Geisel holds a creature he created called Blue Green Abelard.

Theodor Seuss Geisel, better known as Dr. Seuss, is one of the most famous children's book authors of all time. Geisel wrote children's books from the 1930s until his death in 1991. His books are well known for their nonsense words, wild rhymes, and funny drawings of strange creatures. With his books, Geisel

This photograph shows Geisel reading *The Cat in the Hat* to schoolchildren.

created a world of imagination that both entertains and educates children.

More than 600 million copies of Dr. Seuss's books have been sold around the world. They remain

A boy holds a copy of the popular Dr. Seuss book *The Lorax*.

best-selling books, with *Green Eggs and Ham,* *The Cat in the Hat,* and *How the Grinch Stole Christmas!* among the most popular.

Although Geisel did not think it was necessary for books

Vocabulary Box

The PULITZER PRIZES are awards given to American reporters, writers, and musicians.

for children to teach a lesson, many of his books contain strong messages. *The Lorax* is about the importance of protecting our planet, while *Oh, The Places You'll Go!* offers encouragement to those starting out in life. In *I Can Read with My Eyes Shut!*, Geisel wrote, "The more that you read, the more things you will know. The more that you learn, the more places you'll go."

Geisel received many prizes for his children's books. He won three Caldecott Honors, which are awards for artists of picture books for children. In 1984 he received a PULITZER PRIZE for all he had given toward "the education and enjoyment of America's children and their parents."

CHAPTER TWO

A PLAYFUL IMAGINATION

Theodor Seuss Geisel was born on March 2, 1904, in Springfield, Massachusetts. His father, Theodor Robert Geisel, and his mother, Henrietta Seuss, were children of

Here is a view of Geisel's hometown of Springfield, Massachusetts, from about 1850.

German **IMMIGRANTS** who came to the United States in the 1800s. Young Theodor, called Ted by friends and family, had an older sister named Marnie.

Vocabulary Box

IMMIGRANTS are people who travel to a country to live there.

Ted's father was president of his family's brewery, a place where beer is made. His mother's family owned a bakery. When she was a child, Ted's mother listed the pie flavors for the customers at the family bakery using rhymes. When Ted and Marnie were young, their mother sang the same rhymes to help her children fall asleep. Ted believed he got his love of rhymes from his mother.

Ted's mother also supported his love of drawing. Ted's father helped run the local zoo so Ted got to spend a lot of time there. After a visit to the zoo, he would come home and draw animals on the wall.

Geisel is shown working on clay models of some of his characters.

His animals never ended up looking like the animals at the zoo. They had long ears or strange feet. Ted liked to take parts of one animal and draw them on another, creating tigers with wings or giraffes with elephant ears. Ted's sister, Marnie, said that there was a cartoon by her younger brother in every room.

A firefighter reads *The Sneetches* to students during a Read Across America program.

The Geisel family faced **PREJUDICE** during World War I (1914–1918) because they were German. Many countries, including

Vocabulary Box

PREJUDICE means having unfriendly feelings about a person, group, or race.

Quick Fact

One of young Ted's creations, called the Wynnmph, had ears that were 9 feet (2.7 meters) long.

the United States, were fighting against Germany in the war. Ted was bullied at school and sometimes had rocks thrown at his head. Ted remembered these experiences when he wrote stories such as *The Sneetches*, which warns against judging others based on their looks or background.

Ted was not a star student in high school like his sister, but he did well in English and enjoyed writing jokes for the school paper. He decided to go to Dartmouth College in Hanover, New Hampshire.

CHAPTER THREE

A YOUNG CARTOONIST

At Dartmouth, Ted Geisel worked on the *Jack-O-Lantern*, the college's humor magazine. His classmates loved his very funny stories and drawings. By his junior year, Geisel was the **EDITOR** of the magazine. After Geisel graduated from Dartmouth in 1925, he went

This photograph of Geisel was taken when he was a student at Dartmouth College.

Vocabulary Box

An **EDITOR** is someone who gets a book or magazine ready to be printed. An editor also makes changes and corrects mistakes in something that is written.

to Oxford University in England to study to become an English teacher. He was not interested in his schoolwork and spent much of his time in class drawing pictures of imaginary creatures.

At Oxford, Geisel met Helen Palmer. Palmer saw Geisel's drawings and told him that he should be

Geisel and his wife, Helen, spend time outside their home in La Jolla, California.

working on cartoons rather than studying to become a teacher. Palmer graduated from Oxford, but Geisel dropped out to work on drawing cartoons. They both returned to America, and Geisel sold his first cartoon, to the *Saturday Evening Post,* in 1927. He married Helen Palmer that same year.

As a cartoonist Geisel began using the PEN NAME Dr. Theophrastus Seuss, which he soon shortened to Dr. Seuss.

Vocabulary Box

A PEN NAME is a name used by a writer instead of his or her real name.

Along with working on his cartoons, Geisel worked in advertising. He made a lot of money in advertising, but it was not the work he wanted to do.

In 1936 Geisel and his wife took a trip to Europe by ship. On the trip home, he started coming up with rhymes to match the loud noise the ship's engine made. Those rhymes were the beginnings of

Geisel created hundreds of characters during his long career as a children's book author.

Quick Fact

Some of the cartoons Geisel drew at Dartmouth were of imaginary creatures such as a catbird and a dogfish.

And to Think That I Saw It on Mulberry Street. The book tells the story of a boy whose imagination turns a "plain horse and wagon" into a circus parade. Geisel sent *And to Think That I Saw It on Mulberry Street* to more than 20 publishers, but none of them wanted the book. Finally, Vanguard Press published the book in 1937. Geisel's next children's book, *The 500 Hats of Bartholomew Cubbins*, was published in 1938.

CHAPTER FOUR

BEGINNER BOOKS

Although Geisel's life was going well, he was worried about the state of the world. World War II (1939–1945) had begun in Europe, with France, Great Britain, and other countries fighting against Germany, Italy, and Japan. Most Americans did not want to get involved in the war, but Geisel feared Germany's plan to take over all of

Geisel spent many hours drawing the pictures for each one of his books.

Europe. He was also upset that German leaders were killing millions of Jews.

Geisel started publishing more serious cartoons to try to convince Americans to get involved in the war. After the United States entered the war in 1941, Geisel joined the Army. He was sent to Hollywood, California, to work on films to help train the troops. Two of the films Geisel made during the war later won **ACADEMY AWARDS.**

After the war, Ted and Helen settled in La Jolla, California. Geisel spent much of his time working on children's books, often writing from 9:00 PM until 2:00 AM the following morning. He would sometimes write 200 lines to come up with four that he thought were good enough to be put in one of his books. Between 1947 and 1956 Geisel published eight books, including *Horton Hears a Who!* In this book, Horton the elephant works to

Vocabulary Box

ACADEMY AWARDS are prizes given for achievement in the film industry.

19

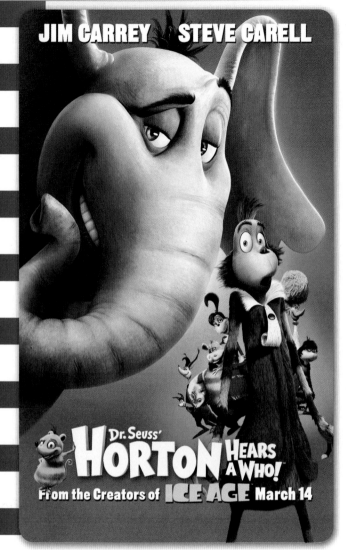

JIM CARREY   STEVE CARELL

DR. SEUSS'
HORTON HEARS A WHO!
From the Creators of ICE AGE March 14

Horton Hears a Who! was made into a movie in 2008.

keep the tiny Whos of Whoville from being destroyed by other animals because he believes "a person's a person no matter how small."

In 1954 Geisel saw an article about how boring most books used to teach reading were. He set out to write a book to entertain children as well as teach them the words they needed to know. Geisel spent over a year working on the book and nearly gave up. It was only when he rhymed "cat" and "hat" that he found his story. *The Cat in the Hat* tells the story of a talking cat that comes to play with two children on a rainy day. The cat makes a mess, but he is able to clean things up before the children's mother gets home.

The Cat in the Hat entertains children while teaching them how to read.

The Cat in the Hat (1957) sold so well that Geisel and others started Beginner Books, a company that published books for young children. That same year he published *How the Grinch Stole Christmas!*, which was later made into a television special and feature film. *How the Grinch Stole Christmas!* is about a mean creature named the Grinch who tries to ruin Christmas for the Whos of Who-ville by stealing all of their presents, food, and decorations. When he hears

Geisel works on a sketch of the Grinch, who was one of his favorite characters.

the Whos enjoying themselves even without their presents, the Grinch decides to join in the fun.

After the success of *The Cat in the Hat*, his editor challenged Geisel to write a book using only 50 words. The result was *Green Eggs and Ham*, published in 1960. *Green Eggs and Ham*, one of the best-selling children's books of all time, is about a creature named Sam-I-Am who tries to convince the main character to eat green eggs and ham. At first the main character does not want to eat the eggs and ham, but when he finally tries them he likes them.

Quick Fact

After moving to La Jolla, Geisel taught a yearly children's workshop at the La Jolla Museum of Art.

Geisel published more than a dozen books between 1956 and 1967. These included *Yertle the Turtle and Other Stories, One Fish Two Fish Red Fish Blue Fish,* and *The Sneetches and Other Stories.*

Sadly, Helen Geisel died in 1967. The following year Geisel married Audrey Dimond, who was a longtime friend and who had two young daughters.

Students are shown reading *The Sneetches and Other Stories* to their classmates in this photograph.

CHAPTER FIVE

GEISEL'S GIFT

During the 1970s and 1980s Geisel continued to write funny books for children. He also took on more serious subjects. In 1971 Geisel published *The Lorax*, which introduced the Once-ler, a creature who

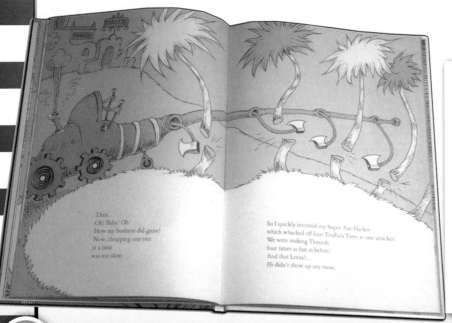

Then...
Oh! Baby! Oh!
How my business did grow!
Now, chopping one tree
at a time
was too slow.

So I quickly invented my Super-Axe-Hacker
which whacked off four Truffula Trees at one smacker.
We were making Thneeds
four times as fast as before!
And that Lorax?...
He didn't show up any more.

These pages from Geisel's book *The Lorax* show Truffula trees being chopped down. The story reminds readers that it is important to take care of the environment.

ruins the land by cutting down all the Truffula trees. When only one Truffula seed remains, the Once-ler gives it to a boy, hoping he will plant more trees. The *Butter Battle Book* (1984) deals with the fight between the Yooks and the Zooks about whether to eat bread with the butter side up or down. The fighting gets worse and worse, with each side creating a bomb that could destroy the other.

By the 1970s, Geisel's health began to fail. He came down with an illness that led to him having trouble seeing. In 1983 doctors told Geisel he had cancer. The last two books published in Geisel's lifetime were *You're Only Old*

Geisel signs copies of *You're Only Old Once!* at a bookstore.

25

Once! (1986), which was written for adults, and *Oh, the Places You'll Go!* (1990), which is a popular gift for those who have finished high school or college. *Oh, the Places You'll Go!* is about the ups and downs people face on their way to a successful life.

Theodor Seuss Geisel died of cancer in 1991 at the age of 86. His **LEGACY** lives on in the many books

First Lady Michelle Obama reads *Green Eggs and Ham* to students in Washington, D.C. Read Across America Day is held each year on Geisel's birthday, March 2.

Quick Fact
Lark Grey Dimond-Cates, Geisel's stepdaughter, created the sculptures in the memorial sculpture garden.

he wrote and the ways in which he changed children's literature. The National Education Association honors Geisel by holding its Read Across America Day on his birthday, March 2. Read Across America Day is part of the Read Across America program, which tries to get schoolchildren to take a greater interest in reading.

Audrey Geisel (*second from left*) visits the Dr. Seuss Memorial Sculpture Garden in Springfield.

In 2002 the Dr. Seuss National Memorial Sculpture Garden opened in Geisel's hometown of Springfield, Massachusetts. The garden features

A girl reads *What Pet Should I Get?* during a visit to a bookstore. The book was published in 2015.

bronze sculptures of Geisel and some of his most well-known characters, including the Cat in the Hat, the Lorax, and the Grinch. In 2015 it was announced that the Amazing World of Dr. Seuss museum would open in Springfield in 2016.

After his death, Geisel's widow, Audrey, found some of Geisel's lost stories at their California home. Several of these have been turned into books, including *The Bippolo Seed and Other Lost Stories* (2011), *Horton and the Kwuggerbug and More Lost Stories* (2014), and *What Pet Should I Get?* (2015). Geisel's books remain as popular as ever, and his characters will continue to entertain children for many years to come.

TIMELINE

1904: Theodor Seuss Geisel is born on March 2 in Springfield, Massachusetts.

1927: Geisel sells his first cartoon, to the *Saturday Evening Post*, and marries Helen Palmer.

1937: *And to Think That I Saw It on Mulberry Street* is published.

1943: Geisel joins the U.S. Army's Information and Education Division.

1957: *The Cat in the Hat* and *How the Grinch Stole Christmas!* are published.

1958: Geisel and others start Beginner Books at Random House.

1967: Geisel's wife, Helen, dies.

1968: Geisel marries Audrey Stone Dimond.

1975: Geisel is honored by Dartmouth College 50 years after his graduation.

1978: Geisel publishes *I Can Read with My Eyes Shut!*, a story in which the Cat in the Hat talks about how fun reading can be.

1984: Geisel receives a Pulitzer Prize for his contribution to children's literature.

1990: *Oh, the Places You'll Go!* is published. It is the last book published during Geisel's lifetime.

1991: Geisel dies at the age of 87.

1998: The Read Across America program begins.

2002: The Dr. Seuss National Memorial Sculpture Garden opens in Springfield, Massachusetts.

2013: Audrey Geisel discovers more of her husband's lost stories and plans to have them turned into books.

2015: *What Pet Should I Get?* is published. Springfield Museums reports that it will buy Geisel's childhood home at 74 Fairfield Street in Springfield.

GLOSSARY

ADVERTISING The business of calling attention to goods or services to make someone want to buy those goods or services.

CONVINCE To cause someone to agree to something.

CREATURES Living things that may be real or imaginary.

DECORATION Something that makes things look nicer.

ENCOURAGEMENT Words that makes someone feel more hopeful, positive, or brave.

GRADUATE To finish school and receive a degree.

POPULAR Liked by many people.

PUBLISH To prepare and produce a book for sale.

RHYMES Words that have the same sound or end with the same sound.

SCULPTURES Pieces of art that are made by carving or molding clay, stone, metal, or other matter.

SERIOUS Important, not light or casual.

WIDOW A woman whose husband has died.

FOR MORE INFORMATION

BOOKS

Guillain, Charlotte. *Dr. Seuss*. Chicago, IL: Heinemann Library, 2012.

Pascal, Janet. *Who Was Dr. Seuss?* New York, NY: Grosset & Dunlap, 2011.

Waxman, Laura Hamilton. *Dr. Seuss*. Minneapolis, MN: Lerner Publications, 2010.

WEBSITES

Because of the changing nature of Internet links, Rosen Publishing has developed an online list of websites related to the subject of this book. This site is updated regularly. Please use this link to access the list:

http://www.rosenlinks.com/BBB/Seuss

INDEX